This book belongs to

....

Quarto is the authority on a wide range of topics.

Quarto educates, entertains and enriches the lives of our readers—enthusiasts and lovers of hands-on living.

www.quartoknows.com

© 2019 Quarto Publishing plc

First published in 2019 by QEB Publishing,
an imprint of The Quarto Group.
6 Orchard Road, Suite 100
Lake Forest, CA 92630
T: +1 949 380 7510
F: +1 949 380 7575
www.QuartoKnows.com

A CIP record for this book is available from the Library of Congress.

ISBN 978-0-7112-4935-6

Based on the original story by A. H. Benjamin and Nick East
Author of adapted text: Katie Woolley
Series Editor: Joyce Bentley
Series Designer: Sarah Peden

Manufactured in Guangdong, China TT012020
9 8 7 6 5 4 3 2 1

MIX
Paper from responsible sources
FSC® C016973
FSC
www.fsc.org

Reading Gems

Not Now, Mom!

QEB

Mom and Lenny were in the kitchen.

Mom asked Lenny to help.

Not now, Mom! I'm eating.

Too late! It rained, and the washing got wet.

Dad and Lenny were in the yard.

Too late! The store was closed.

Tina asked Lenny to turn off the water.
Too late! The bathroom got wet.

8

Lenny and Terry were at the store.

Lenny and Terry were late again.

The family were fed up.
Lenny did not help.

We must help Lenny.

He was never on time.
He made everybody wait.

Mom was watching television.

Will you come and play?

14

15

Dad was reading in the yard.

Lenny was too late to play at the park.

Tina was in the bathroom.
Lenny could not go in.

Not now, Lenny!
I'm taking a shower.

Tina made Lenny
wait and wait.

Lenny was fed up. Everybody made him wait. He did not like it.

21

The family went to the park.
Lenny was on time!

He was never late again.

Story Words

bike

Dad

eating

kitchen

Lenny

Mom

park

rain

reading

store

television

Terry

Tina

washing

water

yard

Let's Talk About Not Now, Mom!

Look carefully at the book cover.

Who is on the front of the book?

Can you tell from the characters' expressions what they are feeling?

In the story, Lenny is asked to help with everyday chores.

How do you help around your house?

What jobs do you like doing? Which ones don't you like?

Lenny is always saying "not now."

Why do you think he keeps putting off helping others?

What happens when he doesn't help?

How do you think Lenny feels when he realizes what it is like to wait?

Have you ever felt the same way Lenny does?

What lesson do you think Lenny has learned by the end of the story?

Did you like the story?

Fun and Games

Read the sentences, then match them to the pictures.

1. Tina was in the bathroom.

2. Dad was reading in the yard.

3. The family were fed up.

4. Mom and Lenny were in the kitchen.

Sound out the letters, and read the words. Find the first letter of each word hiding in the picture.

mom   wet   park   store

Your Turn

Now that you have read the story,
try telling it in your own words.
Use the pictures below to help you.

READING TOGETHER

- When reading this book together, suggest that your child looks at the pictures to help them make sense of any words they are unsure about, and ask them to point to any letters they recognize.

- Try asking questions such as, "Can you break the word into parts?" and "Are there clues in the picture that help you?"

- During the story, ask your child questions such as, "Can you remember what has happened so far?" and "What do you think will happen next?"

- Look at the story words on pages 24–25 together. Encourage your child to find the pictures and the words on the story pages, too.

- There are lots of activities you can play at home with your child to help them with their reading. Write the alphabet onto 26 cards, and hide them around the house. Encourage your child to shout out the letter name when they find a card!

- In the car, play "I Spy" to help your child learn to recognize the first sound in a word.

- Organize a family read-aloud session once a week! Each family member chooses something to read out loud. It could be their favorite book, a magazine, a menu, or the back of a food package.

- Give your child lots of praise, and take great delight when your child successfully sounds out a new word.

Level 2

Lenny and Terry were at the store.

Come on. We must go!

Stop! I'm shopping.

Lenny and Terry were late again.

School

Short sentences ✓

Simple vocabulary ✓

Some repetition ✓

Pictures and words support one another ✓